SHUTOUT

orca sports

SHUTOUT

JEFF ROSS

ORCA BOOK PUBLISHERS

Library and Archives Canada Cataloguing in Publication

Ross, Jeff, 1973–, author
Shutout / Jeff Ross.
(Orca sports)

Issued in print and electronic formats.
ISBN 978-1-4598-1876-7 (softcover). — ISBN 978-1-4598-1877-4 (pdf). —
ISBN 978-1-4598-1878-1 (epub)

I. Title. II. Series: Orca sports
PS8635.06928S58 2019   jC813'.6   C2018-904873-5
C2018-904874-3

First published in the United States, 2019
Library of Congress Control Number: 2018954079

Summary: In this high-interest sports novel for young readers,
Alex has to figure out who's trying to get him kicked off the hockey team.

*Orca Book Publishers is dedicated to preserving the environment and
has printed this book on Forest Stewardship Council® certified paper.*

Orca Book Publishers gratefully acknowledges the support for its
publishing programs provided by the following agencies: the Government of
Canada, the Canada Council for the Arts and the Province of British Columbia
through the BC Arts Council and the Book Publishing Tax Credit.

Edited by Tanya Trafford
Cover photography by iStock.com/Dmytro Aksonov
Author photo by David Irvine Photography

ORCA BOOK PUBLISHERS
orcabook.com

Printed and bound in Canada.

22 21 20 19 • 4 3 2 1

For Alex, and all the goalies who feel as though they stand alone.

Chapter One

The glove save wasn't perfect. It bounced off my wrist instead of settling into the pocket of the glove. But a quick-moving center had been on a breakaway, so the fact that the puck wasn't in the net was all that mattered. I pushed back to protect the post, wrapping my left arm around it and sealing off any space where the puck might find its way through. The center who'd taken the shot was already in the corner, attempting to dig the puck away from the boards. I swung my head quickly to the

1

side to see if anyone was coming in looking for a one-timer. Sure enough, there was a winger standing a couple of feet to the side of me. No one near him.

Where was my defense?

I looked back in time to watch the forward flick the puck away from the boards. It floated just off the ice. I tried to get my stick on it, but the center had managed to deliver it just slightly out of reach. As it passed my stick I swung off the post, following the puck's motion. The center had his stick pulled back. In a flash the puck was flying toward me. Somehow I managed to get my pad down, kicking the puck out to the other side of the net. I followed it again, having no idea if someone else would be there to hammer it home behind me. A stick came out, and again the puck flew at me. I was sliding sideways and caught it in the chest. It popped up and over me— luckily, clearing the top of the net.

I pushed back again, covering the post. One of my players shot past, flying around the back of the net. Another came and stood on the other side, protecting against a wrap-around. I stood up straight and looked over my shoulder. One of my defensemen, Luke, was holding the forward against the boards. My other defenseman, Aiden, was nowhere to be found. At least, I didn't see him. But I couldn't spend that much time looking. A goalie always watches the puck. It's his only job. To know where the puck is at all times and keep it out of the net.

The puck squirted free, and the other team's center grabbed it and took a wild shot. I caught it in my glove and fell to the ice. I made certain the puck stayed deep in the pocket and didn't come out. There was crashing above me. Everyone shoving around. The other team trying to pry the puck loose before the whistle blew. My team trying to keep these guys off me. The problem is, with all that shoving, the goalie is often the guy who gets hurt. I've been lucky so far. No major injuries. But still, when you're crumpled there on the ice and can feel these big guys getting banged around, it's pretty scary.

Someone shoved me into the net just as a body fell in front of me. The ref was blowing his whistle like mad. The guy on the ice turned to me. "Lucky," he said. I kept my head down, the puck inside my glove tucked in tight to my body. "You're not always going to be so lucky." Then he was gone. Yanked away from the crease and sent flying across the ice.

"You all right, Alex?"

I looked up. Luke was in front of me, a big smile on his face.

"Jolly good, sir," I said.

"Right-o, right-o. Well done, chap," he said, patting me on the head. I can't remember when this crazy pretending-to-be-upper-class-British thing started. Likely when we were little kids, since Luke and I have been playing together since we were seven. Somehow it is still hilarious to both of us.

I slid out of the net and dropped the puck on the ice for the ref. "What happened to Aiden?" I said.

Luke shook his head. "He decided he needed a rest right when that guy got the breakaway."

I glanced over at the bench as the ref skated to the face-off dot. Aiden was sitting beside Travis, the other goalie for West High Thunder. They are the best of friends, and unfortunately, Aiden always wants to prove that Travis is a better goalie than me. Even more unfortunately, Aiden has the power to make me look bad simply by not doing his job. But this time, he'd left me high and dry and everyone had seen it. The coach was reaming him out on the bench.

I glanced at the clock. Two minutes left. We were up 3-1. The puck dropped, and our center, Jake, shot it back to Luke. He bounced it off the boards and out of our zone. I relaxed a little. Watched the play move up the ice. This was the thing about being a goalie. It was like what soldiers talk about—endless periods of utter boredom followed by intense seconds of nonstop action.

With West High Thunder, though, the periods of utter boredom are few and far between. The only time I really get a rest is when Luke and Matt's line is out. They know their job. Sure, they get beat now and then—everyone does—but most of the time, when they are on the ice I am confident I am going to face nothing but routine shots. Things I can easily handle. None of this clean-breakaway stuff or ridiculous cross-ice one-timers.

The play wrapped around the other end and started back toward me. I pounded my hand deep into my glove and glided forward. Then Luke cut in, took the puck clean away from the streaking winger and passed it cross-ice, and Matt popped it out of the zone again. One minute left, and no one was looking to get off the ice. I glanced at the bench and noticed Aiden arguing with Coach Ryan. Coach just shook his head and walked away as Aiden slammed his stick into the back side of the boards.

The play was moving toward me again, and although Luke was boxing the guy out, keeping him to the outside, the player managed to get a pass off to his center. Jake was coming back as hard as he could, but he'd been trapped behind the other net. Which allowed the other team's center to fly up the ice. The puck had settled onto his stick like metal to a magnet. He looked up. I watched his eyes for a moment and saw him looking top shelf. He rolled the puck back on his stick, readying it. Just as he was about to flick it, I slid out and poked it off his stick, over to the boards. Luke came in hard, spun around and sent the puck back up to center ice. Time ran out.

Some people would say it wouldn't have mattered if that one had gone in. We'd already won. We were already in first place. But like I said, all that is totally beside the point. I have one job out here. My game is keeping the puck out of the net.

And I am good at it.

Chapter Two

I didn't say anything to Aiden in the locker room.

I didn't have to.

Coach Ryan was sitting beside him.

I've been pretty lucky with coaches over the years. I've only had one screaming one, Coach Jesse, and that was years ago. He'd get right up in your face and lose it. But he yelled enough that year that we won a championship, so in some people's minds it was worth it. I'd been mostly left alone by Coach Jesse. He was all about scoring goals. He'd expected me to keep the puck out of our net, but understood how difficult a position goalie is.

The hardest position in all of sports, he'd say. Then he'd hit his legs and say, *For the body*. A tap to the head. *But more for the mind*. Back then I'd just played. Nothing really got to me. Not much does now either. But it is sometimes difficult to let it go. The puck's in the net. Everyone's cheering. And you're sitting there thinking, If I'd been an inch that way or moved back to the post faster or kicked out that way...

Then the play gets going again and you hope that it comes at you immediately. Otherwise you stay there thinking about that one save you didn't make. Not the fifteen or twenty you've already made. Just that *one* you didn't. It always feels like a mistake. But the thing is, even if it *was* a mistake, so what? Everyone else on the ice makes mistakes all the time.

The difference is, when a goalie makes a mistake *everyone* knows.

Anyway, Coach Ryan was talking quietly to Aiden. But Aiden wasn't really listening. Travis was right beside him. They always sat like that. Side by side. The team was giving me fist bumps. Some teams I've been on have not exactly made me feel part of the group. Like, there's the *team*—the guys who score the goals and get the glory—and then there's me back there. The wall. One coach I had made everyone play net at least once during practice so they could appreciate what it was like to "just stand there." Most of the forwards ended up sitting on the bench to catch their breath halfway through practice. The defensemen did a little better, but they always returned to the locker room just gulping down water.

"Good game, sir," Luke said.

I put my mask on the bench and started working on the straps of my pads. "To you as well, good sir," I replied.

"Sorry about that mess," Matt said. "I couldn't get back there fast enough."

"Alex took care of it," Luke said. "Wasn't your fault."

"Don't worry, Matt," I said. "I like a little adventure now and then."

"All right, guys," Coach Ryan said, standing. Clapping his hands. "Quiet down a second." Everyone stopped talking, although a lot of the guys kept taking off their gear. The *zzzzz-zzzzz* of straps being unfastened. "Stop and listen, please." The *zzzzz*ing stopped. "That's better. Okay. Good game, guys. That was really good. Good hustle. Good clearing. I think we doubled those guys up with shots on net. But there were still some problems. First of all, we need to have a man in front of their net all the time. Centers, this is your job. Get in there. Make life difficult for the goalie. Get in his way. There were at least a dozen shots the goalie could see clearly. Anyone at this level is going to stop those, no problem."

Coach Ryan walked the length of the room and back. "On our end, same thing. But do just the opposite. Clear that man out. We don't want a guy just standing there, waiting for the one-timer. Defense, you have to move that guy out of there. Put him on his butt if you have to. That's Alex's zone, and it's your job to keep it clear for him."

Luke gave me a pat on the shoulder, leaned over and said, "You don't like big stinky guys in your zone, do you?"

"Hate it," I said. "It's very unpleasant."

"And changes. We can't have any more sloppy changes. They're going to kill us. We had a penalty for too many men on the ice. That's the laziest penalty you can get. When you want off, *get off*. But don't do it when the play is coming straight at you. I don't care if you're completely gassed. You can rest for an extra shift if you need it. But while you're out there, you are going full speed."

He stopped again and returned to the center of the room. "We need one more win, and then we're on to the finals. It's likely the Wildcats will make it to the finals as well. Don't kid yourself—they'll be in the arena watching. Looking for a weakness. Something they can exploit in the playoffs. We cannot give them anything. This is the time of year we need to play our hardest." He clapped his hands. "All right, guys, good game. You should all be proud. One practice this week, and then we'll finish this round on Friday."

We were ahead two games to none, and so far the other team hadn't put up much of a resistance. We hadn't lost to them all season, so I didn't see us suddenly losing three games in a row.

Everyone clapped for Coach. It's what we always did. Even if he came in and spent fifteen minutes pointing out our errors, we'd still clap for him.

Once I had all my stuff off, I packed my bag and started out of the locker room.

"Good game, Alex," said Coach Ryan. He put his hand out, and we did two low fives. Tradition. "See you Wednesday for practice."

"Who's in net next game?" Aiden asked from behind me.

"Why are you worrying about next game, Aiden?" Coach asked.

"Just wondering, that's all."

I don't think Coach answered, though I can't be certain. I was out the door and gone before he could even open his mouth. There's enough drama on the ice.

No need to bring it into the locker room.

Chapter Three

Chloe was waiting in the lobby for me like she always does. She has to skip class to come to the games. Our school administration is normally cool with this. Support the team and all that. But the thing is, Chloe ends up sitting pretty much alone the whole time. She's an arts girl, which means all her friends are arts kids. They don't come to any sports events.

She came toward me and gave me a hug, then quickly stepped away. "You didn't shower," she said.

"I have to get home," I said.

"Chubbs?"

"Chubbs," I replied. Chubbs is our new boxer puppy. My parents are out all day, and Chubbs will destroy the place if we don't keep him in his kennel. The thought of him locked in a cage all day drives me nuts. I hope he'll start behaving someday soon so he can get out of there. But for the time being he spends his time in dog prison, with weekend passes.

"I'll come," Chloe said. She took my stick, and we started walking the few blocks to my house. At fifteen, having a bag on wheels is embarrassing. But most of the other players' parents pick them up from games. I have to lug my stuff home.

"When are you going to get a big contract and buy me a Porsche?" Chloe asked.

"Oh, probably next week." I heaved the bag up a curb.

"Good," she said, "although sooner would be better. I'm just saying."

"You can't even drive yet."

"Ah, but wouldn't it be nice to have a Porsche as your first car?"

"I think that would be like flying first class the first time you got on a plane. For the rest of your life you'd walk by those seats and remember how good it was before cramming yourself in one of the tiny economy seats."

"Not if you never had to stop flying first class," she said. "Or, in this analogy, stop driving Porsches."

I laughed. Chloe has quite the imagination. The thing is, I think about the same things sometimes. What would it be like if I actually became an NHL goalie?

As we got to the door of the house, I could hear Chubbs whimpering.

"Oh, the poor guy," Chloe said.

Once we were inside, the whimpering turned to mad barking. Chloe let him out of the cage, and he went nuts. We were back outside in seconds. He made it as far as my mother's garden before he angled up to a tree and emptied his bladder.

"He's getting better at that," Chloe said.

"Peeing?"

"Not peeing."

"Yeah. Now if we could just teach him that couches aren't for eating, he could have the run of the house." We walked the block to the dog park and let him loose. There was only one other dog there, its owner idly tossing a ball with one of those ball chuckers. Chloe and I sat on a bench. She leaned into me like she does.

"So, good game?" She knew not to ask right away. Win or lose, a goalie's game is often difficult to rate. There've been games where we've won 5–3, and I've been really upset. Like, goal two should not have gone in. Goal three should have been blown dead. I can get pretty worked up about this stuff too. Then there was a game last year where we played this elite team out of Quebec and lost 5–2. But that game was gold for me. I made at least fifteen glove saves in the first period alone. The snipers on the other team actually had to think about how to get pucks past me. Other teams in that tournament had lost by eighteen and twenty goals. So a 5–2 loss for the team was a win for me.

"Not bad," I said. "I got left alone out there a couple of times, but that happens. I'm sure Coach will fix it in practice."

"On to the finals, right?" she said. I liked this about Chloe. She kind of knew what was going on but didn't get hung up about where we were in the standings or what the next game was. She just supported me. I'd heard some girls at the school brag about their high-scoring boyfriends, and it always made me a little sad. I was never left wondering if Chloe liked me because I was on the team or because I was me.

"One more win, then on to the finals."

"Right. One more game." Chubbs ran over, and Chloe scratched him behind the ears. "How are you so freaking cute?" Chubbs closed his eyes for a moment, then backed up and ran away again.

"What about you? How was your day?"

"I had art, drama and music, then skipped math and history to come watch you. So yeah, pretty awesome."

"That sounds perfect."

Chloe sat up straight and turned toward me. "I know you hate these things, but Amy's having a party." I threw my head back and looked at the sky. "It'll be cool though. Ella asked Luke to come. I think she likes him."

"That is a horrible idea," I said.

"Don't judge," Chloe said. "They got paired up in Economics and hit it off."

Luke had said nothing about this to me. But then, we didn't exactly sit around talking about girls.

"Ella goes through guys like I do underwear."

Chloe leaned away from me. "I hope you change your underwear more often than that."

"She dates a lot of guys."

"Still."

"Fine," I said. "I'll go. But I can't promise I'll have fun or anything."

"No one would expect that from you," Chloe said. Then she jumped up and started running after Chubbs.

Chapter Four

The next morning I was called from homeroom to the principal's office. I was still half asleep. After Chubbs and I had dropped Chloe off at her house the day before, I'd gone home, had dinner and then disappeared into endless games of *NHL18*. I don't play any other video games. They just have never interested me. And, to be honest, I don't play *NHL18* that much either. But sometimes when I am dead tired and need something mindless, I'll sit down and do five or six games in a row. I had gone to bed eventually the night before, but it must have been after midnight.

So I looked like death walking into Principal Novak's office. He sat there in his baggy suit, looking at me through his wire-frame glasses. His pencil-thin mustache twitched.

"I don't believe I've seen you in here before, Alex," he said finally. That isn't as impressive as it may have sounded. Novak just took over as principal at the beginning of the term.

"No," I said. I almost said *sir*, but I likely would have accidentally said it with a British accent. And then I would have started laughing. That would definitely not be good.

"And yet here you are," Principal Novak continued.

My head was so foggy that I wondered if I was coming down with something. Like a cold or flu. I mean, I don't work well when I don't get enough sleep, but seriously, I felt just awful.

"I understand you're an artist," he said.

"I'm a goalie," I said, assuming he had me confused with someone else.

"For our team, yes." He nodded, turning to his computer monitor. "But also an artist."

"I wouldn't say that," I replied. I'd signed up for art at the beginning of the year. But that was mainly so I could be in at least one class with Chloe. It hadn't worked out. Our schedules were just too different.

"Hmm," Novak said. Then he turned the monitor to face me. "Well, I'd call this art, wouldn't you? A bit angular for my taste, but still."

On the screen was a blocky robot painting. It looked like it had been done using the stencil I'd made in art class. A robot was the first thing I had thought of when we were given the assignment to create our own stencils. It's something I've drawn since I was a kid, and I still really like it. Plus, I'd known the simple shape would be easy enough to cut into a stencil. But I didn't recognize the background.

It looked like a brick wall.

"Where is that?"

"Oh, come on. You know where this is," said Principal Novak.

I looked again. "I don't have a clue."

"This is on the gymnasium wall. The outside wall, but still."

I looked at the image more carefully.

"Okay..." I said.

Novak tilted his head at me. He looked like Chubbs does when I have a piece of bacon in my hand.

"So would you like to explain how it got there?"

"I have no idea," I said.

"This is your art though," he said, tapping the screen. His finger left a little smudge.

"It looks like one of the stencils I made in art class, yeah. But I didn't do it."

Novak shook his head as though confused. "Okay. Well, Alex, where would we find this stencil then?"

I rubbed at my eyes.

"Are you tired?"

"Yeah, I guess." I thought about it. "The stencil is probably in the art room."

"Not in your locker?" he asked.

"Maybe. But I kind of remember it being in the art room."

"Let's go see," he said, standing. "We'll check your locker first though."

"Okay..." I said. I rose slowly.

"You seem very tired, Alex. Were you out late last night?"

"I might be getting a cold," I said.

I followed him down the hall to my locker. Kids were now on their way to first class, so I got a lot of looks. I tried to brush them off, look away, but when you're following the principal down the hall, people pretty much come to a complete stop to watch.

Novak stood beside my locker and waited for me to open it. I'd already been in there once this morning. So I was pretty surprised to see the robot stencil jammed up tight against the left side. My coat was pushed into the back corner by it. Novak grabbed the stencil and ran a finger along it. A smudge of black paint came off on his finger.

"This is yours, correct?"

"I don't think it was in there before," I said. "I'm pretty sure it was in the art room."

"Really?"

I thought back to hanging up my coat when I'd gotten here. I definitely hadn't pulled the stencil out and then jammed it back in against my coat. But how could it have got in there? No one knew my combination but me. Not even Chloe.

"It wasn't there earlier, Mr. Novak, I swear."

"It wasn't?" Kids were moving slowly past us, like this was the scene of some kind of car accident.

"No. It was pushed against my coat. I would have noticed it." Novak looked into my locker, then back at me. "Like, maybe it was slipped in through the gap."

Novak took the stencil and tried to fit it through the gap. The stencil bent and folded but didn't go through. "That seems unlikely."

"I think it would fit."

"*Very* unlikely."

I looked at the ceiling. "There are cameras here, right?" I said. "Maybe we could check those."

"We could try," he said. "That might clarify things a little."

I rubbed at my eyes again. *I should have just gone to bed last night.*

"Where were you last night?" he asked. Like we were in some kind of cop show.

"Home. All night."

"Alone?"

I almost laughed. But I knew that would only make things worse. "Yeah. I mean, my parents were home, but otherwise."

"I'll check that out as well," he said.

I shook my head in disbelief. "Why would I spray-paint my own stencil on the wall of the gym?" I asked.

"That's a very good question," he replied. "I think you'd better get to class. We'll talk again later. Once I have more of the facts."

I stood there watching him walk away, frozen. What had just happened? Then I felt Chloe's hand on my back.

"What was that all about?"

"I have no idea," I said. "Hopefully, it's nothing."

Chapter Five

I didn't hear from the principal again until Wednesday. Right before practice he called me into his office.

"You'll notice your art has been cleaned off, sir," he said. The *sir* made me laugh. Just a quick exhalation, but he caught it. "Do you find something funny here, Mr. Paterson?"

"No, sir." I inhaled another laugh, because all I could picture was Luke's face. The two of us calling one another "good sir" with our stiff upper lips.

"Destruction of school property is not funny," he said.

It was difficult to take him seriously with that little mustache. What made him think that it looked good? Was he trying to imitate someone famous? It was so thin and small that there were little hairs growing around it.

I could see my robot stencil in the corner of the room, up against the wall. Whoever had used it as a stencil had been sloppy. There was a ton of thick paint on it.

Principal Novak didn't know me, had never even met me prior to this, so I could see how he might be trying to figure me out. Was I attempting to get away with something, or was I actually innocent? I also realized there was no way I could prove I was 100 percent innocent just by standing there.

"What about the cameras?" I asked.

Novak scratched at his face just below his right eye. "Your locker is conveniently out of range," he said. Like he thought

I'd set the cameras up for the school and hatched this plan years ago.

"What about other cameras? Did you see anyone carrying the stencil around?"

"I cannot discuss the movements of other students with you, sir," Novak replied with a sniff.

I managed to stifle the guffaw that time, but just barely.

"You are excused. I understand you have hockey practice."

"I do."

Novak turned back to his computer and started typing, so I let myself out. I rolled my bag into the arena, which was right next door to the school. Someone clapped me on the back. "Good day, sir," said Luke.

"Far from it," I replied.

"Is your life as an urban artist causing you grief?"

"I didn't choose the thug life, sir. It chose me."

"How stupid would you have to be to draw on the school with your own stencil?

And then jam it in your locker? I've known you a while, and you're definitely stupid—I mean, you let people fire pucks at your head—but you're not *that* stupid."

"Thanks for your support," I said. We banged through the doors into the arena. I could hear the Zamboni clearing the ice. When we stepped into the locker room, the first two people I saw were Travis and Aiden.

Aiden looked up, flashed his smirk of a smile and yelled, "Well, look who it is! Alex Paterson—goalie by day, vandal by night." He slapped Travis on the chest plate.

I looked away, dropping my stick onto the rack. There was still a space big enough for me to get all my gear out. Luckily, it was on the far side of the room from Travis and Aiden. Luke sat down beside me. Braden, one of our forwards, was beside Luke.

"Why did you do that?" Braden asked.

"Don't be an idiot, Bray," Luke said. "Alex isn't some crazed graffiti artist."

"It looked cool," Braden said. "Really professional. When I first saw it, I thought it was supposed to be there."

"Now it's just a great big wash of white paint," Zack, another defenseman, said.

"Yeah, they should've left it up," Braden said. "It could have been, like, our mascot or something."

"I'll admit it was cool," I said. "But I didn't put it there."

"I didn't know you had that kind of talent," Zack said, ignoring my words. "When did you become an artist?"

"He had to once he started dating Chloe," Braden said.

There wasn't any truth to that. I've been drawing since I was a kid. The robot has been there since the beginning. I gave him all these different poses. I found him fun and easy to do. I drew other things, of course, but that for sure was my favorite piece.

"I'm surprised Novak didn't kick you off the team," Aiden said. "I heard he was pretty pissed." I didn't respond, which obviously bugged him. "Hey! Can you hear me over there?"

"Knock it off, Aiden," Luke said.

"I'm just saying I thought Novak was a hardnose and we wouldn't see Mr. Paterson here today."

I dropped my pads on the ground and fell into them. I saw Aiden smirk again. I knew what he was thinking—big boys don't have to lie down to get their pads on. They strap them on sitting up. But I like a certain feel to my pads. I like them a little tighter in the knees, and I can never get them tight enough while sitting. I also go through a bit of a routine, even before practices. Down on my knees, strap in, pop up, go back down, pop up. Even if there are people beside me. It wakes my body up and makes me hyperaware of my surroundings.

The door opened, and Coach Ryan stuck his head in. Coach had once played Junior A. He'd even been looked at for the OHL. But eventually he'd decided he wanted to go to school and that the long grind of trying to make it to the NHL wasn't worth it. There was every chance he could've made it too. He was that good. We had all watched the old videos of him on YouTube. But instead of trying for the NHL he'd taken a scholarship at university and gotten his teaching degree.

"Five minutes, boys." He spotted me across the room. "Good to see you here, Alex."

I didn't know why he felt he had to say that, but I wasn't about to ask him in front of everybody.

Chapter Six

Principal Novak was in front of the school the next morning. I didn't know he was waiting for me at first. I just saw him there scanning the crowd. I had my hockey gear with me. Coach had managed to get some extra ice time and wanted to focus on defensive positioning. The snow crunched beneath my feet. It had been a long winter, and everyone was tired of it. Hockey is the only way I get through the season at all. I hate the cold. I had dreams when I was younger of living somewhere warm. Maybe playing hockey for LA or San Jose. Somewhere out on the coast, where year-round you change into your shorts after practice.

I heard my name as I started dragging my bag up the stairs.

"Mr. Paterson, please follow me to my office." Novak turned and walked through the door. He didn't even bother to hold it open for me. I had to struggle with my bag and the door at the same time. My goalie stick banged against my back and then the window as I backed up my bag a little. That was when I saw it. Another one of my stencils had been used to paint a white robot on the front of the school.

I knew where that stencil was though. I took it home from art class more than a month ago. It never sat in my locker. It would have only been in the art room for a month. I dragged my bag to the office. I was trying to pull it through the doorway when Novak reappeared.

"Leave that out there," he said. I didn't want to leave my bag out in the hall. I didn't think someone would steal it. But there was every chance that some joker would move it. Or strap on the pads for a laugh. I wasn't going to leave it in the hallway.

"I'll take it to the equipment room," I said.

I was backing out again when Novak said, "I asked you to leave it there."

"I can't just leave it in the hallway," I said.

"And yet that is what I'm asking you to do, sir." Novak's eyes narrowed.

"Principal Novak," interrupted Maria, the office administrator. "We do have a policy here of not leaving bags or equipment of any description in our hallways."

"Thank you, Maria," Mr. Novak said, clearly irritated with her. "Alex, please take your bag to the equipment room and then come right back." The room was right across the hall. I dragged the bag over there, unlocked the door with my key and put it inside. There were two other bags in the far corner, along with Travis's extra set of pads.

I went back to Principal Novak's office ready to defend myself. But as I opened my mouth, he pointed at a chair.

"Sit down, Mr. Paterson."

I did as I was told. My parents have taught me to have respect for authority figures. Whether you agree with them or not. That includes coaches, refs, teachers and principals. So I sat there silently. I was sleepy again. This time it was because I stayed up late finishing an essay. I should've done it ages ago, but it is always so hard to get started on those things.

Principal Novak interlaced his fingers and stared directly at me. There was a piece of toilet paper stuck to his neck. I guess he'd cut himself shaving. I tried not to focus on it, but it's hard not to focus on something you're trying not to focus on. Especially when it's a little piece of bloody paper.

"Destruction of property is taken very seriously here," Principal Novak said. "It will take Mr. Bell a considerable amount of time and effort to clean off this recent piece."

"Mr. Beale," I said. I shouldn't have. I don't know why I even opened my mouth. But the property maintenance man's name is Mr. Beale, not Bell. He's a good guy who comes and watches our games. He played in goal when he was a kid and often gives me little tricks and hints that he thinks could be useful.

"Pardon?" Principal Novak said.

"Just that his name is Mr. Beale, not Bell," I said. "That's all."

Principal Novak looked quite annoyed. "The paint used in this most recent act of vandalism seems to be of a higher quality than the last. Therefore removal is going to be very difficult, not to mention very costly. Where do you suppose I should obtain the funds for cleaning this, Mr. Paterson?"

I decided not to answer. It felt like a trap. Even saying I didn't know would be a bad idea. In fact, that is very often the trap that people like Principal Novak use. They wait for you to admit that you don't know something so they can tell you how things *actually* are.

"Should I take some funds from the hockey team? Or the art department?" He leaned back in his chair. "I'm trying hard to understand this, Alex. Your grades are excellent. I've gone through all of your reports, and there's been nothing but statements on how well you're doing, how positive an influence you are in the classroom. Some teachers even referred to you as a leader! And yet you are the only one who could have created these paintings that deface my building."

"Anyone with the stencil could've done that," I said.

"That's interesting, Mr. Paterson," he said with a bit of a sneer. "Because as far as we know, you are the only person with those particular stencils."

I didn't reply. The fact was, I had no idea how to explain what was happening, and I knew I just sounded like I was trying to blame someone else.

"I'm not certain what to do here, Mr. Paterson. I'm not sure how to read you. Your records show that you're a very good student and have caused no trouble to the school whatsoever. On the other hand, we have this wanton destruction of school property. Is something going on at home?"

"No," was all I said. I doubted anything else would change his mind.

Novak leaned back in his chair. It made a loud, high-pitched squeal. "I'm not sure how we're going to deal with this situation, Mr. Paterson. But for now, you'd better get to your first class before you're late."

I stood up. I wanted to try one more time to tell him it hadn't been me. But then I realized no one could prove I hadn't been at the school the previous night. My parents start work early, so they both usually go to bed super early. As early as nine o'clock sometimes. The school is only a few blocks from my house. I could easily have snuck out, spray-painted the wall and got home again without them ever knowing. Without anyone knowing.

And even though I hadn't, with the way Principal Novak was treating me, I was starting to wish I had.

Chapter Seven

"Alex," Coach Ryan said as I walked into the locker room that Friday.

"Yeah, Coach?"

"Come here a sec." I leaned my bag beside the door and followed him into the arena. The Zamboni was doing its slow circles. The arena was icy cold, as always, the stands empty. The scoreboard flashed 0–0. This was our warm-up time. The third game of the series was that night at seven, but it was only three thirty now. The arena felt abandoned. Coach Ryan leaned against the glass and looked out on the ice.

"The principal came to talk to me today. He seems to think you've been up to no good lately."

"I have no idea what's going on, Coach," I said. "Someone took the stencils I made in art class and has been using them to put graffiti on the walls here."

"That's pretty much the same story I heard. Except the principal seems to think that someone is you."

"I know he does."

"He asked me what I thought the possibility of your being involved was, and I said zero. There's no way. I don't think he left all that convinced." The Zamboni was doing its final pass. The driver gave us a wave. We both waved back to him. "In the end I told him I'd bench you tonight." Coach Ryan stood up straight. "I didn't tell him it was your turn to sit anyway. He doesn't seem to know that much about hockey.

"The Wildcats are into the finals," Coach continued. "If all goes well, we can be too. If we are, the first game of that series is Monday. I always said we'd give equal time to everyone over the season. But these are the playoffs. I now reserve the right to put in whoever I think will win us the game." He looked over at me, clapped me on the back and then gestured toward the door. "Better get your stuff on."

The practice went well. We scrimmaged for the last twenty minutes, which is always fun. It gives everyone a bit of playing time. A better understanding of how bouncing the puck off the boards works for blowing by a defender, or how people are feeling about receiving and giving passes. My side won 2-1, but it didn't really matter. Coach Ryan was blowing the play down over and over, trying to correct some of our positioning.

I went home, and Mom had a giant plate of chicken with just a bit of sauce ready. Some broccoli, snap peas and the tiniest bit of rice, and then it was back to the arena. I do everything exactly the same whether I'm backup goalie or in nets. The same bending, stretching, up and down—everything. Goaltending is all about routine. I wanted to make certain I was ready to play if I got called in.

It was a bit hard to be on the bench, watching the other team go up three goals in the first period and not being able to do anything about it. I looked to Coach Ryan a couple of times, hoping he'd put me in as relief. But I guess he was letting Travis figure it out. The other team had six goals before we got our first. Their last goal was a weak five-hole that had Travis banging his stick on the post. I wasn't sure why he did this. Was he angry that the puck had gone in? Was he frustrated with himself? If so, why hadn't he bothered to work on his lateral movement during practice that day? The other teams had picked up on his poor lateral pushes early in the season and used this against him in every game they could.

The final score was 6–4. We're not a really high-scoring team but can always be counted on for three or four goals. That means our side can let in no more than two. We never really get blown out. But 6-4 felt like a blowout. Nevertheless, we went onto the ice at the end of the game as a team and skated the circle, our sticks raised high. Back in the locker room, Travis immediately started chirping everyone.

"What was that, guys? Seriously," he said, throwing his helmet into a bag. "A bit of defense would have been useful."

He sounded like his dad. I'd been on junior teams with him. He would come in and yell at all the defensemen, telling them the things they'd done wrong. Yelling at ten- or eleven-year-old kids. Maybe sometimes the defense had let Travis down. But we were at a higher level now. Every single player on this team had pride in what he did. No one was going to throw this game. We didn't have it in us.

"What did I just hear?" Coach Ryan asked, stepping into the room.

"I had no coverage," Travis said. "How many of those were second shots? I make the first save, then they clear the puck. That is how this works."

"That is *not* how this works, Travis. We play as a team. And I felt like we played as a team out there tonight."

"Like a crappy team," Travis said.

Everyone was staring at him. He got like this sometimes after a game, unable to rein in his anger. He would just go on and on.

"Put a cork in it, Travis," Coach Ryan said. A few of us stifled laughter. He had a few of those old-time phrases. "We played a good game." He walked across the room to the board. "We let the guys inside. That's it. Especially on the power play. We need to keep that four-man box. When it falls apart, everything falls apart." He looked around the room. "We're still up two-one in this round. But remember, we are not a team that throws blame around. We back one another up. That's how we've got this far and that's how we are going to keep going forward, understand?"

Everyone nodded to this.

"We go again tomorrow. Let's finish this round and look to the finals." He paced back and forth. It seemed like he wanted to say more, but instead he just opened the door and walked out.

Chapter Eight

I had just stepped out of the shower when I heard voices downstairs. I opened the door a crack and looked out. I could see Mom and Chloe talking. Chloe was in her blue winter jacket, the fake fur still up over her head. I could see her hair was curled, and she'd taken some care working on her makeup. Chubbs was jumping on her and leaving dirty paw prints on her coat. I wrapped the towel around my waist and stepped out.

"Alex! Put some clothes on," Mom called up the stairs. "Get down, Chubbs. Why are you always jumping on people?"

"And hurry up," Chloe said. "I don't want to miss the whole party."

The last thing I wanted to do was go to one of Amy's parties. Amy seemed to believe we should have high-class gatherings. She always had some game planned, or the party had a "theme." But at least Luke would be there too. I threw on a pair of jeans, grabbed a hoodie, then changed my mind and put on a black shirt. I went to the mirror, did some work on my hair, swiped some deodorant on my pits and was downstairs within minutes.

Chloe smiled, then shook her head. "So easy for you guys," she said. "Jump through the shower, put on a shirt and a bit of hair gel, and you're out the door. Five minutes." She threw her arms around me and kissed me on the cheek. "Looking gorgeous."

"I prefer handsome."

"Midnight curfew, correct?" Mom said.

I was fine with this. I didn't need to be out any later. It was only nine thirty, but with school and practice and, honestly, all the stress from people thinking I was some kind of vandal, I was exhausted. "Correct," I said.

The wind was blowing tornadoes of snow around the front yard. It was one of those deadly cold nights. Amy's house was only four blocks away, but by the time we got there we were frozen. The house was warm though. Amy had wineglasses set up, but there wasn't any actual wine visible. Just sparkling juice. We had team rules against drinking. There were a lot of team rules, and they all made sense, but I likely would have stayed in line even if it wasn't a rule. I needed a clear head for the next game.

Luke was already there, leaning against the fireplace with a tumbler in his hand. When he saw me he raised it slightly. I heard him call across the room, "Good evening, good sir!" I ignored him and hung

up my coat. Chloe and I crossed the room
to the fireplace.

"Fancy seeing you here," I said.

Luke shrugged. Chloe and Ella were
deep in conversation. I noticed Ella was
wearing Luke's Thunder jacket.

"I was invited," he said, sipping from his
drink.

"I see you've loaned your jacket out."

Luke blushed a little. "She was cold.
I'm a gentleman."

I decided to let it go. "What's that?"

"They call it sparkling water."

"Oh, do they?"

"It's delightful."

"Well, I think I might go get myself one."
I asked Chloe if she wanted anything. She
said whatever I was having.

The kitchen was a madhouse. There were
three cases of beer on the kitchen table
and a giant box of wine on the counter.
The noise was incredible. It seemed as if
all twenty or so people in the room were
talking at once. I knew a few people and

heard my name called. Some of the kids avoided looking at me directly. I didn't know how to read them. Were they suspicious of me because I was a jock? Were they angry because they thought I'd defaced the school? Or were they jealous because they thought I'd defaced the school *and* was getting away with it?

I couldn't put too much effort into figuring out what other people thought of me. It just wasn't worth my time. So I opened the fridge, got out the sparkling water and went rummaging in the cupboards for a couple of glasses. I managed to find one clear glass and one with Mickey Mouse all over it. Luke would think it was hilarious, especially if I pretended there was nothing weird about it. I set the two glasses on the table and turned around for the sparkling water. Someone bumped into me, and I moved out of the way. It was this kid Georgie. He likes to be called Georgie, not George.

"Hey, Alex, how's it going?"

"I'm good. How are you, Georgie?"

"Fantastic. Hold this for me, would you?"

I put my hand up without thinking, and he slid a bottle into it. I looked down and saw it was a beer. I'm no prude, but I didn't want to be seen standing there with a beer in my hand. I felt like I was walking on thin ice with Coach Ryan as it was.

"I don't want this," I said, trying to hand it back to Georgie.

"I'm not giving it to you—just hold it." Someone else bumped me, and I turned my head for a second, then looked back at Georgie.

"Here, thanks," he said, taking the beer from my hand. I looked down into his little round face. He smiled and walked away. I didn't know why, exactly, but I got a bad feeling.

I poured the sparkling water into the two glasses and then returned to the very calm living room. "Here you go," I said, handing Chloe the not-Mickey Mouse glass.

"Thanks," she said.

"I'm really tired," I said. "Is it okay if we don't stay too long?" Chloe's face fell. I hated disappointing her. I wished I could stay out later and party with her arts friends. But they always excluded me. In their eyes I was a hockey jock. Not an artist. I could have a painting in the National Gallery and they'd still refer to me as Goalie Boy. There was no winning with them. I really liked Chloe, but sometimes her friends were obnoxious.

"I can get a ride home with Ella," she said. She took my hand in hers. "You okay?"

"Yeah. Really, I am. Just seriously tired."

She stretched up to kiss my cheek. "Go anytime you like. I don't mind. I mean, I'll miss you, but no one is fun when they're exhausted."

I talked to Luke for a while. Sat with Chloe and listened to one of her friends go on about a Wes Anderson film. I love Wes Anderson as well, but no one asked for my opinion. If they had, though, they'd probably have changed their minds when they discovered that some jock had the same opinions about the film.

It was just after eleven when I finally stood and said I was going to get going. Chloe walked me to the door. "Get lots of sleep," she said before giving me a kiss and closing the door.

I walked home that night feeling really confused. About Chloe's friends. About the weird thing with Georgie and the beer bottle. The funny looks people had given me earlier. The fact that someone was using my stencils to get me in trouble. Maybe I was just being paranoid, but it felt like someone was trying to ruin my life.

Chapter Nine

I looked more dazed than drunk in the photo. Coach Ryan had it open on his phone, which he was holding in front of me.

"I need an explanation, Alex," he said. The bottle of beer was clearly visible.

"Oh no!" I said. "Where did this even come from?"

"I'm afraid Principal Novak sent it to me," Coach Ryan said. "Is there something going on that I should know about?"

"Nothing, no. I wasn't drinking, honest! I was just holding it for this kid." Even I knew how stupid that sounded. It was the most obvious excuse. Unfortunately, in my case, it was also the truth. I thought briefly of saying something like *It was Photoshopped!* or *It was someone who just looks like me!* Because the truth was just too unbelievable.

"You will have to sit out the next game," Coach Ryan said. "Principal Novak was digging around our rule book and discovered the no-drinking policy. But I would have had to enforce it anyway. You know that."

"Even though I wasn't drinking?"

Coach Ryan tapped his screen to wake it up and held the picture out again. Me, holding a beer. There was no other way to look at it. Two of our players, Miles and Braden, had been suspended for a couple of games for drinking. Now I was being benched, and the timing couldn't have been worse. Travis had managed to win the game on Friday night, and we were in the finals.

"But I'll still play the second game, right?"

Coach Ryan pocketed his phone. We were in the hallway outside the locker rooms. Warm-up would be beginning soon.

"I can't make any promises," Coach Ryan said. "Principal Novak is peeved. He might be making an example of you."

"But I haven't done anything," I said. It felt so unfair.

"I will try to talk to him. But you better be telling me the truth, Alex. I am going out on a limb for you."

I couldn't look at him. "Thanks, Coach," I said. Then I turned and slumped back down the hallway.

I was just going to go home, but instead I put my bag in the equipment room and went looking for Georgie. I could whine about it being unfair. Mope around and do nothing. Let people believe I was some kind of vandal who spent his weekend nights drinking at parties.

Or I could try to set the record straight. I knew Georgie did lighting for the school plays and that there was a rehearsal on. We have an auditorium especially for plays and concerts, along with our regular gym. I eased through the door of the auditorium, making sure not to let too much light inside. Fortunately, I'd arrived during a break. The actors were moving around on the stage. The lights were blinking, and then one settled in a halo on the center of the stage.

I'd forgotten that Chloe had done most of the set design. I wasn't sure what the play was, but the entire back of the stage was covered in paintings of giant flowers, small mountains in the distance, tall grasses along the edges. I could see her style in everything. She'd likely painted the entire thing by herself.

Georgie was lounging in a seat near the light booth. He didn't seem to notice me until I sat down beside him. He pulled earbuds from his ears and looked at me.

"Hey, Alex," he said.

"Hey, Georgie," I said. "Remember the party the other night?"

"Yeah, why?" Georgie said.

"Do you remember when you handed me that beer?"

Georgie kind of screwed up his face and looked across the room as if someone had called his name. "Maybe? It was pretty hectic. Was it in the kitchen?"

"Yeah, it was in the kitchen."

"You weren't drinking," he said.

"I wasn't drinking," I replied. "But someone took a picture of me holding that beer. And that picture made its way to Principal Novak."

Georgie shook his head once. "Ah, man. I'm sorry," he said. "That really sucks."

"It more than sucks. It means I'm currently suspended for the first game of the finals."

"Hockey finals?" Georgie said.

"Yes, Georgie. Hockey."

Georgie inhaled and raised his hands palms up. "So what are you going to do?"

"It's not what I am going to do," I said. "It's what you can do. I want you to go tell Principal Novak that you handed me the beer. And that you never saw me drinking."

"I can't do that," Georgie said.

"Why not?"

"There's a no-drinking policy for the theater team too," Georgie said. "There are two other guys who would love to be running lights here. I want to go to college for TV broadcasting. I need this gig."

"But you were *actually drinking*," I said.

"Sure, but there isn't a picture of me doing it."

I suddenly felt the anger that some of the players must feel when someone's been digging into their ribs, hacking them during the face-off or plowing into them when the refs aren't looking. I kind of wanted to crush Georgie into the wall, but I also knew that would do no good.

"What if I tell him it was your beer?"

He raised his hands palms up again. "I would say I know nothing about it. Alex, seriously, it's just one game, right?"

I stared at him.

"This play starts in three days. If I get booted now, someone else gets to do the whole run. I don't get to come back."

I stood up and stared down at Georgie. His arms moved as though he was readying to protect himself from me. "You're a real piece of work, aren't you, Georgie."

"One game, Alex, and then you'll be back." He raised a fist in the air. "Go, Thunder." He was right about it being just one game. But this was about more than that.

A lot more.

Chapter Ten

The next day started out bad and got worse.

I received a text from Luke in the morning. We had lost the opening game 6-2. Luke was rarely unkind or petty, but after sending me the final score he texted: **Is it really that hard to move left to right?**

I didn't answer. The last two times we'd played that team, I had shut them out. We'd won both games 2-0. They were not a super scoring team, so the fact that we'd lost on Monday by such a margin was surprising.

When I got to school I dropped my gear in the equipment room, then left, locking the door behind me. Something felt familiar. A scrap of memory trying to surface. I stood there for a moment, trying to block out all the noise. I went into the equipment room and stood there for a second, then backed out again. Turned the key in the door. The scrap returned. I opened the door and looked at the spot where I always placed my bag. Then I remembered.

I couldn't believe I was doing it, but there I was, knocking on Principal Novak's office door.

"Alex Paterson, please come in." I stepped in and sat down as Principal Novak walked around me and closed his office door. "How can I help you?"

"I just remembered something," I said. Suddenly I was sweating, and my chest felt tight. "I remember leaving the stencils in the equipment room for at least two nights."

"Okay," Principal Novak said. "And?"

"And that could've been when someone took them. That person could've easily copied them. It would only take a few minutes to draw the outline and cut it out later."

"And who are you suggesting did this?"

"I'm not suggesting anyone in particular. I mean, I don't know—I'm just saying it could've happened."

Principal Novak interlaced his fingers again and nodded his head a few times. "And could it also have happened that you were accidentally drinking the other night?"

"Someone put that bottle in my hand," I said. His little smirk returned. "I mean, someone asked me to hold it for them. I didn't drink, I don't drink, I don't want to drink."

"It seems like there are a lot of people conspiring against you, Mr. Paterson."

"That's the way it feels," I said. I felt kind of choked up, like I might burst into tears any second. There was no way I was going to do that here. I'd stand up and smash something before I started crying in that office.

"And why do you think anyone would want to make you look bad?" he asked.

"I don't know," I said. I had some ideas. But if I gave names, Principal Novak would want proof. And I didn't have any.

"I'm not sure how I can help you, Alex," he said. "You're bringing me hypothetical situations. All I have to go on is concrete proof—a photograph of you with a beer, and the fact that your stencils were used to vandalize property."

I sat there staring at him. I wished I hadn't come in.

"I'm afraid there's nothing I can do for you right now," he said. "I understand that you've been suspended for one game. I hope you learn something from this and take it forward." He turned back to his computer and began typing. I felt worse leaving his office than I had going in. Plus, I had to suffer all the people watching me step out of his office.

I spotted Chloe with Ella, down by her locker, and instantly felt a little better. She gave me a wave. I walked over to her and

69

went to give her a hug. But she backed away and looked over her shoulder.

"What's up?" I asked.

Ella slid away. Chloe leaned against the lockers. "This isn't permanent, Alex," she said. "But my parents heard about everything that's been going on, and they're just not sure what to think right now. They said I should keep my distance from you until this all gets figured out. You know how they're all 'the company you keep defines you' and that kind of stuff." Her eyes began to water. She wiped a tear away. "This is just a break. I'm not going to date anyone else or anything like that. But while we're at school I have to, you know, keep my distance."

I could tell she wanted to hug me, but we were standing outside her mother's classroom. Chloe's parents are pretty strict. The thing is, they don't need to be. Chloe's pretty much the best-behaved kid you could ever imagine.

"You know it's not me, right?" I could feel that heaviness in my chest, but all I could do was sigh. It was either that or start bawling in the stupid hallway in front of everyone. In the end I just kind of hung my head, nodded and walked away.

I didn't see any of my teammates that day. We all had different classes. But even in the halls I did my best to avoid everyone. When I got home, I put a leash on Chubbs and went straight back out to the park. My phone binged. Luke. I stopped at a fire hydrant and read the text.

You good?

No

What's going on?

I don't want to sound paranoid, but I think someone's trying to frame me

That does sound paranoid. Who?

Someone who could get those stencils...someone with something to gain if I don't play.

As far as I knew, I'd never really peeved anyone off. I mean, I was friendly with pretty much everyone. I kept my distance from some people, but that was mostly because we didn't travel in the same circles.

I think it has to be Travis and Aiden. The words felt true as I wrote them. I'd been thinking it for a while.

What?

It's all that makes sense. I left the stencils in the equipment room once. They could've made copies...

Why?

Travis wants to be the hero

So far, that is a long way from what's going on

His belief in himself extremely outreaches his actual ability

LOL. A lifetime of being told he's the best and receiving medals for showing up

There's no way I can prove it though. Someone has to confess

Do you have both stencils now?

No. One of them is missing

Then whoever it is will likely do it again

You're right

We have to catch them in the act

Video them

I don't want to believe it's those two. We're a team!

I don't either
We have to catch this paint bandit in the act
Sounds like a plan
ltr
ltr

I lay on my bed going over everything that had happened. Who could it be if not Travis and Aiden? It could be someone else on the team. Or anyone else with a key to the equipment room. The teachers all had them. Mr. Beale. Principal Novak. The more I thought about it, the crazier the ideas got. Why would a teacher want me kicked off the team? The only one I could think of was Chloe's mom. She'd never been thrilled about Chloe having a steady boyfriend. But I'd never done anything to make her dislike me, as far as I knew. I just couldn't picture her out in front of the school, spray-painting a robot onto the wall in order to frame me. I didn't have the same trouble picturing Travis and Aiden.

Chapter Eleven

Principal Novak was waiting inside the front doors of the school the next morning.

"You were asking us about our cameras before, Mr. Paterson," he said.

I didn't want to talk to him. I didn't even want to raise my head in the hallway.

"Before you ask, I was at home all night," I said. I knew there must be some spray-painted robot around here somewhere. I hadn't seen one coming in, so it had to be on the back of the building.

"May I borrow your key for a moment, please?" Principal Novak said.

"What key?"

"The one you have for the equipment room." I pulled my keychain out and held up the equipment-room key. He studied it for a moment, then started walking. I followed him because I figured that was what I was supposed to do. We walked to the equipment room, and he opened the door. Without stopping, he crossed the room to another door. He had to shift a couple of bags out of the way before he was able to unlock that one. He opened it, and we stepped through.

I had never really thought about where that other door went. There was always stuff in front of it. So I was actually pretty surprised to discover we were standing backstage in the auditorium. The stage was dark, but I could see the set design Chloe had created. When my eyes adjusted to the light, I felt sick instantly. In the middle of the set were three giant black robots painted over Chloe's beautiful scene.

"I would never do that!" I said. "That's Chloe's. She painted it all by hand."

"I don't often get into student relationships and such. But it's my understanding that until very recently you and Miss Donovan were a couple," Principal Novak said.

"Well, yeah, with all the stuff that's going on...But I would *never* do something like that. Ever. Not to her work."

"That's where you draw the line? You wouldn't vandalize your friend's work, but the rest of the school doesn't deserve the same respect?"

"I didn't do *any* of it." I was tired of it all. And angry. Nobody believed me. And whoever was after me had destroyed Chloe's work. The play opened in only three days. Enough was enough. I had to get to the bottom of this. I turned around and walked back through the door.

"Mr. Paterson, we are not done here!" Principal Novak yelled. I kept walking. "I need an explanation for this," he called.

"So do I!" I yelled back. The problem was, Principal Novak only had one suspect—me.

I had everyone else.

I told Maria I was going home and left. My parents were at work, so I had the place to myself. I spent most of the day trying not to think about what was happening. But that was impossible. I watched a movie. I played some NHL18. I waited for the day to be over so I could go to the warm-up and get ready for the playoff game that night.

At three thirty I got a phone call from Coach Ryan. "Alex, I'm just going to tear the bandage off here. Principal Novak won't let me put you in tonight."

"Why not?"

"He says you walked away from him today and then skipped school."

"He just can't even consider that it's anyone but me doing this stupid graffiti," I said.

"Well, the evidence is there. I'm not saying I think it's you, but I can understand how someone else might."

I felt the same way. The only way to prove my innocence was to catch someone else red-handed, like Luke had suggested.

"I want you at the game tonight."

"If I'm not going to play, why would I bother?"

"I want the whole team there. You can watch from the stands, but I want you in the locker room before the game."

I had no idea why Coach would do that to me. The last thing I wanted to do was sit and watch my team get beat again.

"I don't know if I can do that, Coach," I said.

"It's not a suggestion, Alex. I expect you to be there." I was about to respond, about to tell him no way, when he quickly said, "See you tonight," and hung up.

It wasn't like I was going to call him back. Besides, there had to be some reason he was asking me to do this.

It felt strange going into the locker room without my gear. I walked in and sat beside Luke.

"Hey, buddy, how are you?"

"Jolly good, old chap," I said. But it didn't feel right.

"What's going on?" Luke asked quietly. I could hear the nervousness in his voice. Across the room Travis was strapping on his pads.

"Coach wanted me to come," I replied.

Jordan Frederick, the junior goalie, was suiting up beside Miles. He looked nervous as well. Even though he was just backup, there was always a chance he was going to have to go in and play against these bigger, stronger guys.

"Big game, guys," Coach Ryan said as he stepped into the room. "We can either tie it up or go down two nothing." He crossed the room with his hands behind his back.

"I asked Alex to be here to try and clear up some issues." He looked at me and then across the room at Travis and Aiden. "By now you all know what's been happening. Alex was suspended from the last game because there was a picture circulated on social media that appeared to show him drinking at a party. Whether this is true or not is still up in the air, but the principal has also been dealing with a number of incidents of vandalism at the school. All evidence seems to point to Alex. Therefore, unfortunately, Alex will not be playing or placed in a backup position tonight." Coach crossed the room again and stood close to Aiden and Travis. I hadn't said anything to him, but maybe he was thinking the same thing I was.

"Alex has told me that he was not drinking at the party and that he is not the one damaging school property," Coach continued. "I believe him, and I would sincerely hope that no one here is attempting to discredit one of his teammates. We are on this incredible run because we've always been a team."

He walked away from Travis and Aiden and stood in the center of the room. "Does anyone have anything they would like to say?" He looked around the room. I kept my head down. "No one has any information that might be useful?" Still nothing.

He nodded, then switched gears. "This is a best-of-five, as you know. We're only down one. That's not that much. The problem is, we're down at home. It will be tough if we have to go into their arena down two games. But I don't see that happening. I saw a good effort in the last game. But effort isn't enough. We need to be smart. We need to think our way through this game. I don't want to see any more drop passes. Those cost us at least two goals. I don't want to see anyone trying to skate the entire ice. No one here is a one-man show. I want to see people in front of our net. I want to see pucks cleared, and I want to see us going back to the basics. I want us to play good, hard, clean hockey. We spent far too much time in our end in the last game, and we cannot afford to do that again."

Coach checked his watch. "Okay, boys, see you out there," he said, and then just like that he was gone.

Chapter Twelve

It was beyond strange sitting in the stands. A lot of kids had come out to watch. Mostly guys who'd played house or rep before but didn't want to be on the high-school team. Other kids were there as well. The stands were pretty full. And up in the top right corner, slightly away from everyone else, sat Principal Novak. I went to the lower left, giving myself as much distance from him as possible.

We started out well, going up two-nothing on a couple of quick goals in the first three minutes. Both of them were beautiful. One was a snap shot from the slot, the other a backdoor jam. Thinking like a goalie, I couldn't fault the Wildcats netminder for what happened. It looked to me as if the Wildcats had come in with some serious confidence that hadn't truly been earned. Halfway through the first period, the Wildcats coach called a time-out right after Matt iced the puck. It seemed a strange thing to do.

At least it gave our guys a chance to rest. We had been running around in our end a little bit. But then I could see the coach holding his board up and drawing out a plan. His top line came back out, but he'd replaced one of the defensemen with another winger. They lined up in our end. The winger he'd put in defense caught the puck cleanly off the face-off, took two steps to the side, then jutted back one extra step and fired it in.

Travis didn't have a chance.

There were two big bodies in front of him. Another guy there ready to tip it in.

You don't see a lot of crashing the net in these types of games, especially with that many skilled players. Which is exactly why our guys were caught outside. They were defending the other two forwards, who had placed themselves in positions that were virtually useless. The only way this play could've gone wrong for the other team was if Travis had managed to kick the puck far up the ice to one of our wingers, who would then have had a clear breakaway.

Travis skated in a circle. I noticed he looked up at me before going back to his crease. I decided to move. It had to be annoying, if not intimidating, to have the other goalie watching your every move. For another player my presence might have been more of a boost of confidence, but not Travis.

Not now.

The Wildcats still had their top line on, although they had now replaced the forward with another defenseman. They won the face-off cleanly and immediately drove the puck into our end. Luke swept it away from the winger and went in for a hit. The winger managed to dodge and, at the same time, pump the puck directly out in front of the net. Their center was there to hammer it toward the empty part of the net. But Travis caught it with his glove. It was a great save. If this had come later in the game, you might have called it a turning point. But this early in a period, it was just what had to happen.

I hadn't been at the first game—had only heard the final score. But tonight Travis was honestly playing his butt off.

As the Wildcats lined up for the face-off, I saw the center talking to his wingers. He put his hand out in front of him and moved it side to side. I knew what he was saying. They were going to try to get Travis moving laterally. It was the only way they could score on him if he kept making glove saves like that.

Travis was skating around his net, so he wouldn't have picked up on this. I wanted to bang on the glass. Tell him what was happening. These guys were playing well.

They were good at moving the puck back and forth across the ice. If our defense got running around, the Wildcats would have an open shot.

The Wildcats lost the face-off. Zack took the puck around the back of the net, then reversed it, sending it up the wing to Miles. He got it out of the zone.

We played in their end for the next minute and a half. That doesn't seem like long, but we managed four good shots on net. None that rattled the goalie at all. None that went in. But as long as you have the lead and are playing at the other end of the ice, a hockey game can feel pretty easy.

Zack took a huge shot from the blue line. Their goalie kicked it out to the boards and directly onto the stick of a forward. He came racing up the ice. He cut a little to the left, just enough to make Travis move to cover the angle, then quickly shot back to the right and lifted the puck up, over Travis's pad and into the net. And there we were, tied at 2–2.

From where I sat I could see how the air had been taken out of our team. Their heads were hanging. Their shoulders were down. When he returned to the bench, Zack tried to get everyone going. Coach walked around quietly, arms crossed. He couldn't be angry about anything that was happening on the ice. I'd like to say I would've easily made that stop. I was always able to go from right to left quickly. I would've had my glove there right where that puck went in. But it was a tough shot to stop, and Travis had almost got it.

The buzzer rang to end the first period. The players all skated to the bench. Coach brought the board down and started drawing things on it. I moved back down to the far left of the stands. I wanted to be able to stare directly at the other goalie when the second period began. If nothing else, maybe I could figure out a few of his moves. Spot his weaknesses.

Halfway through the second period the game was still tied. All our shots were coming from way outside. Their defense was doing a good job of keeping people pinned to the boards, forcing us to consistently cycle the puck around the outside. Round and round they went, never getting into the slot. Then one of their forwards tripped on his own feet and went down. Jake, our big but fast center, wheeled around the defenseman and lifted a nice soft wrister into the top left corner: 3–2.

Before the teams returned to center ice, I saw Coach Ryan pointing at the blue line. There was still half a game left, and he wanted to make certain his players were thinking defense first.

We'd played this game before. You get up a couple goals, then settle in and frustrate the other team as they try to get through the neutral zone. The problem with that is, you always have to be clean. You can't make any simple mistakes. It does eliminate a lot of the more complicated errors that can happen. There aren't any back passes or fancy moves. You play a three-zone game, stop them as they come through the neutral zone, bring it into your own end, then pass it back up and settle in for a shot. One guy fore-checking. The danger is that you keep thinking defensively until one guy thinks offense and goes for the big goal. If he misses, the puck is right in your end, and you're trapped.

Somehow, while I was thinking about all this, that was exactly what happened. Braden went for a beauty shot, but the goalie got down, pumped the puck away with his stick and landed it dead on the stick of one of his defenders. They got a quick snap up to a center who'd just stepped onto the ice. That left only one of our guys back. The center managed to use our defenseman as a shield. He took a shot between his legs, which trickled in as Travis was sliding across the crease in the wrong direction.

We finished that period tied 3-3.

The third period was full of heavy hitting. Players being mashed into the boards at every chance. Both coaches seemed to have the same strategy—wear the other team down. Scare them off the puck. Shuffle it out in front of the net. Have someone bang it in. There were no breakaways. No beautiful cross-ice passes. Just grinding, brutal hockey. Both goalies made the saves they had to make. Travis made a beautiful blocker save, kicking the puck way up above him. When it fluttered in the air, he kept his eye on it and caught it square in his glove.

I wished I could've been out there. I wanted to be able to do something. But looking at it logically, Travis didn't let any in during the third—I couldn't have done anything more than he did. So when the game ended in a 3–3 tie, I somehow felt calmer. Maybe I had misjudged Travis. Sure, he let in the odd weak goal, but he'd stood strong during this game. Maybe he'd just had more bad games than some other goalies. Or maybe he was finding his groove.

There was no time available for overtime. When this happens, they go straight to a shoot-out, just like in the NHL. The Wildcats shot first. They put one of their big wingers in. He skated up slowly, stickhandling the whole way. Then he darted one way and tried a backhand. Travis got his stick down and just managed to nudge it aside. The arena filled with applause. Jake took our first shot and flicked it cleanly over the goalie's outstretched glove. The noise in the arena grew in volume. I was up on my feet with everyone else.

The other team put in a defenseman next. It seemed strange at first. He took about three quick steps in and then hammered the puck as hard as he could. It lifted just high enough to get over Travis's blocker side pad. The netting in the goal blew out on the back. The puck had so much speed on it that it rolled back out through Travis's five-hole as he fell down onto his butt.

The noise in the arena subsided.

Miles was up next. He tried a deke move to then go one-handed, but the goalie held his ground. He poked the puck away before it even got near him. The Wildcats put in their top-line center. He had a wicked shot, but he didn't use it. Instead he skated far over to one side and then cut back. As soon as Travis had pushed to the left, moving toward his butterfly, the center did a quick cut back and lifted the puck easily into the empty side of the net. The arena fell mostly silent except for the cheering of the other team. Just like that, the Wildcats were up two-nothing for the series.

I got to my feet and left. I knew I should go down to the locker room and talk with everyone. But I didn't want to feel the heavy weight of another loss. Especially if I was going to play the next game. The pressure was on.

Chapter Thirteen

Two days later, I heard my name at the end of the morning announcements.

"Finally, could Alex Paterson please come to the office. Thank you, everyone. Have a good day." All the kids in my homeroom looked at me. At this point I figured no one knew what to think. There were so many different "truths" out there. One rumor I'd heard was that I'd gone over some kind of edge when Chloe broke up with me. As far as I was concerned,

we weren't broken up. We were just keeping our distance to please her parents. This rumor also didn't explain the first graffiti, which had happened before this supposed breakup. There were other rumors, but I ignored them. I was the same guy I'd been two weeks earlier—except I wasn't. When you have someone actively trying to ruin your life, it's kind of hard to just act normal and carry on. You get consumed by it.

"Take a seat, Mr. Paterson," Principal Novak said when I stepped into his office. Another kid was in there already. Andrew Gerard. I'd known him since grade school. We'd never gotten along. Not for any particular reason. We were just very different personality types. Andrew was fiddling around on his phone. I couldn't tell if he was playing a game or texting someone. I sat down on the chair next to him. Novak came around from behind his desk and took a seat.

"Alex," he said.

What, no snarky *sir*?

"Mr. Gerard has something to tell you."

Andrew put his phone down and looked up through his stringy hair. "Yeah, like, sorry and stuff," he said.

"You might want to elaborate, Mr. Gerard," Principal Novak said.

"Okay, it was me who took that picture at the party," he mumbled. "And I posted it on, like, Instagram and Snapchatted it too. And I guess I did it because I thought it would be funny."

"I feel the intent might've been more malicious than that, Mr. Gerard," Principal Novak said.

"Maybe. I mean, I just don't know why everyone cares so much about the stupid hockey team. Someone told me that you're, like, really important to the team and that, like, without you they always lose. Everyone would be so embarrassed, and I wanted to see that."

I stared at Andrew. He never once looked at me.

"And you're sorry for these actions?" Principal Novak prompted.

"I already said that. Yeah, I'm sorry."

"Mr. Gerard has confirmed that he never saw you drinking. This doesn't necessarily mean you weren't, but the only proof I had was the single bottle in your hand. Now I know it was not yours and had been handed to you." Novak looked a little uncomfortable. "Therefore, the suspension for the next game has been lifted."

I'd had no idea I was going to be suspended from *another* game.

"Thank you," I said. I immediately regretted it. I really wanted to say, *I told you so*. I wanted to say, *Everything you think about me is wrong*. I wanted to say, *This hasn't been me since minute one, can't you see it?* But Principal Novak lived on "truth." The truth was, I hadn't been drinking at that party. Nothing more, nothing less.

I felt a little different in the hall. I didn't look different, and no one else would notice anything had changed, but I felt a little lighter. I still didn't think the principal was suddenly going to believe everything

I'd been telling him, but it was a start. If I could just figure out who was behind the graffiti, maybe Novak would be ready to see other possibilities.

I saw Chloe with a bunch of people and walked up to her.

"How are you?" she said. Her friends all stepped away.

"Andrew Gerard just came forward to say that he took that picture at Amy's party. He deliberately set me up. He thought it would be funny if I got kicked off the team."

"What a jerk," she said.

"My thoughts exactly. I don't think it's going to change your parents' minds or anything. I don't even think it's changed Principal Novak's mind. But it's something to support the idea that I am still the same person I was before."

Chloe's eyes welled up. "I know you are, Alex. It's just such a mess."

I wanted to give her a hug. But then I spotted her mother coming down the hall and decided to not cause her any more difficulty.

"I'd love to see you in the stands for my next game," I said.

She nodded as she wiped at her eyes. "This is all so stupid," she said as I backed away. "But it'll all be over soon. Right?"

"I hope so," I said.

I have a private goalie coach I go to see now and then. My parents usually give me a bunch of lessons as a gift at Christmas and on my birthday. I hadn't been to see Dave in a while, but he greeted me with the same smile he always did. He asked me how my season was going. He knew we were in the finals of the playoffs. I told him I had had a good season with three shutouts and a very high save percentage. We worked on some basic moves. I felt like I was warming back up to playing. It wasn't like I'd been out that long, but with any break from practice or games, you lose a few things. Things you're never supposed to forget.

About halfway through the lesson Dave started talking about a game he'd had years ago when he played for Princeton.

"There were these two big guys on the team. They played for Cornell. They never played clean. They'd run me, bump me and hack at my glove when I caught the puck. They'd even run me into the post whenever they got a chance. Some of this garbage got them penalties. But they thought it was worth it in a playoff series. The thing was, they really got into my mind. That was their job, right? Make me afraid to do my job. But I didn't want to feel afraid, so I started feeling angry instead. Then I wanted revenge. I wished I was a forward and could hammer them into the boards."

"Did you get through it?" I was doing my slides, making sure my lateral movement was perfect. That my chest was high, glove out.

"Not entirely. I still worried that they were going to run me. That I'd get injured. But somewhere in there I stopped hating them. So when one of them came flying up to the net and took me out by the knees, I did not take the opportunity to bring my stick right down on his open throat. Instead, I rolled over him and skated away.

"He called me a coward, but they knew I'd won. I wasn't playing cheap. I wasn't going to give in to their way of doing things. I wasn't going to play the game that made me that angry and frustrated."

"The mental game," I said.

"Playing net is a mental game. More than any other position in sports. You have to be able to let things go."

I went home that night and had my customary dinner, then went to bed. I tried to think like Dave. I still believed it was Travis and Aiden behind everything—I couldn't think of anyone else. But by thinking that way I was no better than Principal Novak. Plus, it was true what I'd said to Luke. I didn't want it to be those two.

So who else could it be? And more important, why?

Chapter Fourteen

The next game was in the Wildcats' building. Therefore, the cheering would be when *we* got scored on, when *we* got hit, when *their* goalie made a big save. There'd be silence when we scored. I was okay with this, but then, you *had* to be okay with this. Anyone who waits for favorable conditions is never going to get anything done.

Travis didn't seem upset to be on the bench. He'd done his best, and it obviously hadn't been good enough. But he still seemed to have a bit of a "let's see if this guy can do any better" attitude. Like I said before, our goalie tandem was not the best. Normally you'd trust one another. Normally you'd become each other's best friend. No one else really understands what a goalie goes through.

I knew Aiden would play as hard as he could. He didn't want to be the one falling down as a puck went in.

I roughed up my crease, and we stood while they played the anthem. I kind of like that moment at the beginning of the game. The bit of quiet between being in the locker room and being out on the ice. The anthem was just piped in here. Someone pressed *Play* and away it went. We didn't have official singers or anything like that. As the anthem finished I focused on one spot on the ice. My focus remained there until I could see nothing else. Then I dropped my helmet, banged the posts and settled in.

The Wildcats came out firing. I guess this was their game plan. Take as many shots as possible. They were coming from everywhere, which, honestly, was good for me. A lot of shots drifted in slowly. I wasn't facing any absolute rockets, just the kind of stuff you get in practice. There was nothing challenging for the first five or six minutes. Our team slowly picked up the pace. Trying to push the play a little. The problem with going full-out like the Wildcats had been doing was, you get worn out quickly.

I had to put a lot of things out of my mind. All these ideas about who was trying to discredit me, about Chloe sitting in the stands alone, about how I hadn't played in a while. Most of all, how we couldn't lose another game or this was all over. We deserved to win the championship.

We got our first goal right before the first intermission. Matt sent in a rocket from the blue line, and Jake tipped it in. It was an absolutely beautiful thing to watch from my end of the ice. The noise in the arena had been deafening before. But it dropped off to near silence after that goal.

We went into the second, and the Wildcats fans started their chant. The players came out flying again, looking for the equalizing goal. They were taking shots from all over the place. The thing was, I could see every puck. It seemed like each play was a Hail Mary. The hope that maybe, just maybe, the puck would drift in somehow. That might've worked in past years, but at this level there was no hope.

They fired it in so many times that I started working on just pumping the puck out as far as I could—directing it up the boards and out to the blue line if possible. I was trying to send one of our players on a breakaway. We had to keep the points locked down. We couldn't be moving around a lot. The call from Coach Ryan was to play good, clean hockey. If one of our plays was broken up, we backed up, settled into the neutral zone and held them back.

It worked. Most of their shots ended up being dump-ins. They were trying to get the puck into our end, waiting for one of us to make a mistake. The whole second period went that way. The puck getting dumped in hard, rimming around the boards, then squirting back out into the neutral zone.

There were only fifteen seconds left when Jason scored. He cut across the ice, looked like he was going to pass, then ripped one right up into the middle of the net. The goalie didn't stand a chance. He'd already pushed off and was drifting across, looking to cover the open side. I felt for him. Short-side goals always suck.

"We're playing a defensive box from now on," Coach Ryan said at the bench between periods. "Four men squared, one man chasing. Don't let them get shots, and if they do, make sure they're far out and no one is in front of our net. Understand?" We all nodded. We'd played this game before. The box is a defensive move used mostly for penalty kills. But when you have that fifth guy to chase the open player, it makes life very easy. It's not easy to break out and score, but being up two-nothing, we weren't really looking to score again.

It wasn't long before the Wildcats understood that we were just going to lay back, and they began firing from the points, then crashing the net. I had to make a number of glove saves, but most of the pucks ended up down on the ice. As long as I kept my stick covering the five-hole, everything just bounced away. Our focus was to clear the puck as quickly as possible, so the Wildcats didn't get that dirty goal they were after.

I started to breathe regularly again as the clock ticked down to the final seconds and the play was in their end. We weren't really looking for a goal. I could tell our players were just checking the clock. Miles waited until there were only five seconds left, then took a shot. The other goalie caught it with his glove, held it, waited for the buzzer to sound and skated to the bench. My players surrounded me, patting me on the head. The Wildcats had tried the same thing on me as they had on Travis. Moving me side to side. But I had my lateral game down. I could push, dig in and go right back the other way all day.

"One down," Coach Ryan said when we got to the locker room. "Two to go." Both

Travis and Aiden congratulated me on my win. It was gracious praise—and it felt well earned. I told Travis I'd had an easier time than him. No bouncing pucks, no tricklers that scoot one way, then the other. Just clean, straight shots. But when I went home that night I knew without a doubt that I'd be in for the next game.

Chapter Fifteen

Saturday night I went to a movie with my dad. Normally I would have been doing something with Chloe, but with our relationship on hold, my time was open. Dad must've noticed that there was something going on with Chloe and me. He wasn't going to broach the subject directly though. He drove quietly, asking a few questions and telling me about his day. Then, in the darkness of the theater, we were both able to simply be silent.

We'd gone out for tacos before the movie, so we went to the later showing. It didn't get out until eleven thirty. I went straight to bed afterward.

The next morning we awoke at nine to a banging on the door. I was curious about what was going on but not curious enough to get out of bed. Then Mom called me downstairs. I threw on a pair of track pants and a sweatshirt and came down. There in my front foyer was Principal Novak. Chubbs was in the hallway, growling at him. Novak was all bundled up in a big black winter jacket. He held a tablet in his hand.

"Mrs. Paterson, I'm very sorry to have interrupted your Sunday morning," he said, "but there's something I think you should see." He held the tablet up. "Can we look at this quickly?"

"Certainly," Mom said. Then Dad was there, in his plaid pajama pants and old skater shirt.

"Let's go into the kitchen," Dad said. "I just made coffee. Can I tempt you?"

"That would be great," Principal Novak said. He looked at me. I hadn't said a word. He looked really smug.

We went into the kitchen and Dad got a cup down. He asked Principal Novak if he wanted anything in his coffee.

"Two sugars, please," he said. Dad handed him the coffee, and he slurped at it. "Thank you, Mr. Paterson." He woke up the screen on the tablet. I could see there was a video there. It was dark, a hazy light above a wall.

"Can I ask what this is all about?" my dad asked.

"This was taken last night," Principal Novak said. "You'll recognize our arena." He pressed *Play*. There was no sound. Just glitchy second-by-second video. At first there was nothing—just darkness. Then two figures arrived. I noticed one of them was wearing a Thunder team jacket. Everyone on the team has the same one. Some people had put their names on them, but I never had.

The four of us leaned over the video.

One of the figures put a stencil on the wall, brought out a can of spray paint and quickly filled in the open space in the middle. Whoever it was then shifted the stencil slightly to the right, angled downward, and spray-painted again. The figure moved the stencil and spray-painted a third time, then pulled it from the wall. Then the two of them took a quick look at the art before leaving the way they had come. I had to admit that from an artistic standpoint, the stencil looked pretty cool. It appeared that the robot was falling, crashing to the ground and flattening out there.

"So you caught the guys? Who are they?" I asked.

Principal Novak looked at me, his face blank. He shook his head. "Alexander, it's obviously you and an accomplice," he said.

I looked at the video again. There was a time stamp on it: 10:45 PM.

Dad spoke before I could. "That would be a good trick."

"How so?" Principal Novak asked.

"At ten forty-five last night we were in the movie theater. The two of us together." Dad left the room briefly. He came back a moment later with the two torn-off ticket stubs. "I can attest that my son and I were together from five o'clock until almost midnight, when we got home. I locked the door. Alex went to bed. Now, I can't promise you he didn't go back out after midnight—we're pretty heavy sleepers here—but that doesn't matter. This happened at ten forty-five. He was sitting right beside me then, watching a superhero movie."

Principal Novak looked like he might be sick.

"But the team jacket," he said. "The stencil. All of it. This person's even the same height."

"Can we see it again?" I asked.

Novak was stunned. He was sure he'd come here with absolute proof. He pressed *Play*, then gulped from his coffee as the video reran. I watched closely, squinting at the screen, and saw something I thought I'd seen before. At first it freaked me out, but then I looked at the figure. It was almost as tall as me.

And whoever it was had long black hair.

"Did you get one of your friends to do it?" Novak asked.

"Like I said from the beginning, it wasn't me. I had nothing to do with any of it. I wouldn't even think of vandalizing school property. And I would have to be an idiot to spray-paint on the side of the arena after we won again last night. Why would I want to get suspended? My team needs me."

"But why would someone want to do this?" I could see that it was going to take some time for Principal Novak to process this new evidence. He made his way back to the front door, his jacket still on. I had thought I might get an apology. But I guess he was still trying to figure out how I could be in two places at once. He opened the door.

"Again, I am sorry for disturbing you," he said.

"You don't seem sorry," my mom said. "Alex says he did not vandalize anything, and yet you don't believe him."

"Who would admit to something like that?" Novak asked.

"And Alex doesn't drink either," my mom continued, ignoring Novak's whiny reply. "He told you what really happened."

"Him holding the bottle was proof enough for me," Novak said.

"Holding is not drinking." Novak opened his mouth to reply but Mom cut him off. She picked a shoe off the floor. "If someone were to take a picture of me right now, would they suspect I was eating this shoe?"

"That is hardly a logical comparison—"

Mom shook her head. "Well, it seems to be your kind of logic."

"I have always had an open mind," Novak said, stepping outside. He couldn't wait to get out of there. *Go, Mom!*

"So I'm assuming this puts an end to the suspensions and to your suspicion of Alex?" my dad said. It was more of a statement than a question.

"In regards to this particular incident, I am sorry," said Principal Novak. "I'm sure you can see how I was deceived."

"And the others?" Dad said.

"I have no proof for or against Alex's complicity in these vandalism charges. But I can confirm there will be no consequences for Alex regarding this incident."

Dad shook his head. "Well, thanks for dropping by," he said and closed the door. He turned to me. "That guy's a bit of a knob, isn't he?"

"A bit!" said Mom.

"Yeah, that's an understatement," I said.

Chapter Sixteen

Chloe was waiting inside the arena with a couple of friends before our warm-up time. They quickly peeled away from her when I came in. I told her about Principal Novak being at my house that morning.

"It doesn't matter. I knew it wasn't you all along," she said. Her hands were covered in paint. She was wearing her white painter's shirt as well. Ella and Brittany were with a couple of other girls, all of them paint spattered.

"Have you been redoing the sets all day?"

She nodded.

"You must be exhausted."

"The girls have been helping me, but I don't think it looks quite the same as it did before."

"I'm sorry," I said.

She reached out and grabbed my arm. "It wasn't you."

"I know, but I'm sorry it happened."

"My parents still aren't convinced," she said. "Honestly, I haven't even talked to them about this. But I know it will turn out okay."

It was awful not being able to hang out, to be together. I thought about Chloe a lot. At the same time, I was in the middle of the playoffs, and I likely wouldn't have been able to spend that much time with her anyway. I had to keep my head in the game.

"I have to go to practice. Will you be in the stands tonight?"

"Yes," she said. "Good luck." She looked around quickly and gave me a kiss before returning to huddle again with her friends.

The game that night had a different feel to it. The Wildcats came out slow and steady. I figured their coach had decided to play a different kind of game. I could see that they had changed up their lines as well. Instead of having one heavy top line, they'd distributed their three biggest scorers across the first three lines. Whenever the puck went into their end, their defense would go for a hard pass up the boards, the wingers sitting up higher than normal. Our guys caught on to this fast enough and shifted on the boards to intercept the passes.

We didn't change our lines. Didn't change our game plan. We were going to keep trying to clog up the neutral zone and spring one of our wingers. I was thinking offensively as well. If I was able to send the puck far up as the Wildcats were coming into our zone, we would always have one of our wingers sitting high, waiting to accept it. It was a different game as a goalie. I had to make the stops, but I was also looking to press the play. I had to note who was standing high, who wasn't coming all the way back into the zone, who was doing that little half circle to get turned around and wait for a pass.

The first goal came midway through the second.

The play had been in the Wildcats' end for a while when one of their forwards threw his arm up and started skating to the bench, looking for a change. Which was when Matt and Luke were able to settle into a fast back-and-forth, and Luke hammered the puck low-stick side. It wasn't a beautiful goal, but it did the trick.

We were up one–nothing.

It totally took the air out of the arena. Coach Ryan always pushed us to think of every game one at a time. We weren't thinking of bringing this series home. The problem with all sports is that the crushing feeling of defeat far exceeds the joy of winning. Winning is expected, and defeat is never supposed to be an option.

The remainder of the second period played out with some heavy hitting, poor passes, takeaways and just general frustrated play. I made ten saves. I smothered the puck when I could to slow the game down and take the excitement out of the arena. We ended the second as we had the first, up one-nothing.

Their first goal came at the forty-five-second mark of the third. I could see it was a set play once it happened. The forward didn't try and pull the puck back on the face-off. Instead he rushed Jake, jammed him slightly forward and pushed the puck ahead. One of the wingers cut in, taking the puck out of the open ice and blowing it by me high-stick side.

I might've been too far out. Maybe I hadn't cut off the angle right either. I went through all the possible ways I could have stopped the puck. And then, as the cheering carried on in the arena, I let them all go.

We didn't change our style. We played the same way, holding tight in the neutral zone and pushing for that spring-out goal.

It was five minutes into the third when the Wildcats managed to break through our defense. This time it happened when Aiden had jumped off the ice. No one had been ready to go on the ice to replace him, which meant I was facing a two-on-one. The Wildcats forwards passed the puck back and forth. Braden sprawled out on the ice, trying to block the pass, but their left wing got a nice saucer pass up and over him, right onto his other winger's stick. I didn't have a chance. And yet, somehow, I got my toe on it and just managed to bump it to the corner. We were still tied, and this was now a fifteen-minute game. That was all I had to think about. We had fifteen minutes. One minute after another. I had to make every stop that came near me. Push every puck away for fifteen minutes.

I knew I had to protect myself from dirty goals. These guys often tried that. They dumped one or two guys right in front of the net and tried to shovel one past me. There was always hacking on my gloves, jamming up my pads. So when the puck came into my feet and I lost sight of it, I had to scramble.

Zack was back, but he's not a big guy, and it was hard for him to try and shove everyone else around. He got elbowed, and the ref didn't do anything about it. Once Zack went down beside the net, the two forwards immediately started hammering at the puck.

Matt came back and took one of them out. The puck was just sitting there in front of me. I was down in my butterfly, staring at my stick and trying to protect the five-hole. I knew if I stood up quickly to try and jam it away that I'd be exposing too much of the net. But I couldn't just stay there. I watched as the Wildcats forward brought his stick up. I tried to judge where the puck was before falling to the ice. Somehow it popped out from beneath me, over to Miles, who passed it up to Jason. He shoveled it over to Jake. Jake only had one defensive player to get around, and he did that quickly. The defenseman spun around and caught Jake's foot. But Jake managed to scoop the puck up and lift it just over the Wildcats goalie's shoulder. He slid into the boards, arms raised in victory.

There were two minutes left. The Wildcats pulled their goalie. He was halfway to the blue line when the puck dropped. They won the face-off, and he skated hard to the bench while one of their forwards popped over the boards and onto the ice. By the time they got set up in our zone, there was only a minute and forty-five seconds left.

I was ready for the onslaught.

I had to make saves around bodies. Blocker saves, glove saves, stick jams to the corners. I got the play stopped by falling on the puck, which left the puck drop in our end. Somehow we won the face-off but couldn't get it out of our zone. The clock had ticked down to forty-five seconds by the time they got set up and were shooting on us again. But I had Luke and Matt out with me. They would hold the fort, and although they would probably get tired, I knew they were going to play perfectly positional hockey. The only shots that were going to get through would be long bombs.

I couldn't make any mistakes. I couldn't kick the puck up the boards and hope that one of our players would get it. I had to stop the play, if at all possible. I could do that for the next forty-five seconds.

As it turned out, that wasn't what happened. I never got hold of the puck. Every time I managed to go down, the puck was swept aside and shuffled to the boards. Our guys were looking more and more tired. In the last five seconds, one of the big Wildcats wingers came floating up. He had the puck on his stick. I knew what he liked to do. Top corner, blocker side, every time. But what if he changed his mind? What if he decided to keep it on the ice, try a five-hole? I took a chance and cheated to the blocker side, hoping to shut down as much of the net as possible.

He surprised me.

He went glove side. I stretched, got my glove up just in time, caught the puck and held my glove to my body as I fell to the ice and waited for the buzzer to sound. The Wildcats players came in and hammered at my glove, even though it was held tight to my body. The refs didn't blow the whistle until the buzzer sounded, and the period was over. We were going to game five.

Chapter Seventeen

Our next game would be Tuesday night. So on Monday night, on a hunch, Luke and I went to the school. The night was bright and clear and warmer than it had been. There is a maintenance shed on the property that grants a clear view of the school. We could see all of the high school, the arena and even the community center. We'd been there a half hour when Luke started getting antsy.

"No one's coming," he whispered.

"Give it a minute," I said. "Or like, twenty."

He huddled into his winter jacket and knocked snow off a pile of wood.

We didn't have to wait another twenty minutes. In fact, we didn't even have to wait another ten. Two figures moved across the soccer field and stopped at a little bunch of trees near the back wall of the school. They waited there for a minute, then stepped out.

"That's Ella!" Luke said.

"Who's with her?" I said.

"I don't know."

I'd come to believe that whoever was trying to frame me had to be from a different high school. But I hadn't been able to figure out how would they have managed to get inside the school to get my stencils. Or how they would have managed to get a Thunder jacket.

But Ella, of course, had taken Luke's jacket when they started "dating" and hadn't returned it.

I got my phone out, ready to record them. "We have to wait until they start spray-painting. Then we can walk toward them as we're filming. You yell at them, and when they turn around we'll get their faces."

"Forget that. Let's go over and confront them right now," Luke said.

"We have to film them doing it first," I said. "After that it doesn't matter. As long as we see them doing it and get their faces on video."

I turned on my phone's video recorder and started walking in their direction. In an audible whisper, like a documentary film-maker, I said, "This is Alexander Paterson. I'm walking toward the west side of our high school, where two people have arrived with one of my stencils and are now vandalizing the wall of the building."

They must've heard our footsteps, because all of a sudden they stopped, turned around and dropped the spray can to the ground.

"What are you doing here, Ella?" Luke asked.

"What are *you* doing here?" Ella replied.

"You stole my jacket, and now you have someone doing this to...what, frame us?" Luke said. He stepped forward and spun the other figure around. I'd never seen the guy before. "Who are you?" Luke asked.

The guy didn't respond. I moved up close to him to make certain I got a good shot of his face.

"Give me my jacket." Luke pulled on the guy's arm until the jacket fell off.

"I don't get it, Ella," I said. "Why would you do this to me?"

She looked defeated. The guy took off running.

"Hey, get back here!" Luke yelled.

"Don't worry about him, Luke. I'm sure Ella will tell us who he is."

Ella looked like she wanted to run as well.

"Seriously, why would you do this?" I said.

"Because Chloe deserves someone better than you, Alex. Someone who isn't just a dumb jock," Ella said.

"What do you mean?"

"She needs to be with an artist. Someone who's going to bare his soul to her."

"I'm an artist," I said, then felt stupid defending myself to her.

"You drew one robot once, and then you made a bunch of stencils from it, and that's it."

I felt like defending myself again but decided not to bother. Ella wasn't going to believe that I had tons of drawings and paintings. That I spent hours drawing. That I didn't talk about it because it was simply something I enjoyed doing. No, in her mind, to be an artist you had to debate art, learn about all the masters, be part of a crowd that discussed it endlessly.

"I can't believe you would do this, Ella. Do you know how much trouble you've caused me? How close our team came to losing?"

"Oh, sports. Who cares about a bunch of jocks chasing a puck around the ice?"

"I do. The team does. Lots of people do. It matters."

"Well, art matters too, but people don't come out cheering for it."

"People can like both, right?" I said.

Ella held out the stencil. "You may as well take this."

I shook my head. "No, you hold on to it." I turned and started walking away.

Luke caught up with me immediately. "That's messed up, man," he said.

"She must really hate me," I said.

"I never really thought she liked me either, to be honest," said Luke. "It always felt like a bit of an act. Now I know why. People sure are messed up."

"Or maybe they just love the drama," I said.

"That's even more messed up!"

Chapter Eighteen

Luke came with me to Principal Novak's office. There was no way I was going to go alone. I still felt as though I needed the video plus at least fifteen people who had seen the event and another twenty who had heard Ella admit to what she had done. Maybe some kind of theatrical reenactment too, to make certain Principal Novak actually believed me.

I was still baffled by it all. Ella wanted her friend to have a different boyfriend so badly that she would have done anything to make it happen. It wasn't even about me, really. It was about her making decisions for her friend.

"This is compelling evidence, Alex," Novak said. He looked at Luke. "And you say you were there for this?" We had just gone by a part of the video where Luke was on the screen.

"We went because we had a feeling someone was going to do something before the big game tonight."

Principal Novak stared at the screen. "I would never have imagined something like this from Ella Jansen," he said. "Her grades are excellent. She's a model student."

I didn't point out the irony of that statement. I was an excellent student. My grades were great. And yet, I'd still had to prove I wasn't a drunken vandal.

"She says it right there in the video. It was her and this guy all along," I said.

"I just find it very hard to believe. Who is the boy?" Principal Novak asked. He leaned back in his chair.

"I have no idea," I said. Neither of us had ever seen him before. Thing was, it didn't matter. I was bringing Novak proof that I'd had nothing to do with the vandalism. Someone else had admitted to doing all of it. I didn't know why I was still sitting in his office. Oh, wait. Yes I did. I was waiting for an apology. He'd cost me so much, simply because of his suspicions.

"Well, I guess that is that," Principal Novak said. He handed my phone back. "Please send me a copy of that video. I will have a discussion with Ms. Jansen."

It seemed like that was it. We'd been dismissed. The matter was over. Luke stood, but I stayed where I was.

"That's it?" I said.

"The matter's closed," Principal Novak said. "I'm sorry you had to go through this, Alex."

"That's not an apology," I said. My parents had taught me to be respectful, not just of people older than me, but of everyone. But Novak had put me through all this because he had never given me the benefit of the doubt. He'd always thought he was right and that I was to blame. He'd shown me no respect, not even bothering to dig into any of what had happened. *He* had put me through it. But he still was not apologizing.

"I'm not sure what you want from me, Mr. Paterson," he said.

"I want you to say you're sorry," I said.

"I just did."

"You just said you were sorry that I had to go through this. Not that you're sorry you *put* me through this."

Novak's face tightened. "I was following the evidence. That's all," he said. "Put yourself in my shoes. Who would *you* think had been doing these things?"

I stood up. I wasn't going to get anywhere. I didn't even know what I was expecting. An announcement over the PA system? Him saying to the whole school, *I was wrong, Alex Paterson was right, all should be forgiven?* Yeah, right.

"I would believe someone when they told me something," I said. "I would at the very least investigate what they were saying. I would try to find out if there was some other explanation."

"You think I would have figured out that this had something to do with young people dating?" Novak said. Everything seemed beyond him. "I followed the evidence, Alexander. That's all I did. That was my job."

I decided to leave it there. He was never going to change his mind. I wasn't even certain that an apology would do me any good anyway. Plus, I was starting to get angry. I didn't want to get angry. I didn't want to walk out of there feeling like I needed to punch something.

Luke gave me a shot on the arm as we stepped into the hallway. "That was ballsy," he said.

"What?"

"Demanding an apology," Luke said.

"Well, he made my life a nightmare." The morning announcements were playing as we stepped into homeroom and slid sheepishly into our seats. Even though we'd been with the principal, we both were embarrassed to be late for homeroom. Not that our teacher made us feel that way. Mr. Davis was always cool about these things. He assumed that people ran into difficulties. He didn't assume that people were late just because they'd stayed up half the night playing video games and then couldn't make it to school on time. If Mr. Davis were principal, he might not have believed me outright, but he certainly would've looked into what I was saying.

The announcements went on as usual—clubs, a special talk during the lunch hour, the Thunder's final game that evening. They wrapped up with a request for Ella Jansen to come to the office.

Luke looked at me. I shrugged my shoulders. I figured it was about as close to an apology as I was ever going to get.

Chapter Nineteen

The game that night should've been one of the best of the year. A five-game series final almost always is. But in the end, it was just a defensive battle. We went up one-nothing on a sweet play between Jake and Miles at the end of the first period. With neither team really able to get control in the offensive zone, most of the game was just ringing the puck around the boards, someone trying to get hold of it, then running headlong into the wall of the other team.

I had maybe four touches on the puck that entire period. A couple of stick saves, one glove save to stop a puck that likely wasn't even going in and then, for us, this one goal off a little rush. That's the way hockey works sometimes, although it doesn't take much to step up and suddenly get a goal out of nowhere.

The second period was more lively. There was a lot more back-and-forth. A lot more blocked shots. What was coming at me was usually pretty straight-forward. Someone hammering it from the blue line or whiffing it toward net from the boards. There was only one time that it actually got hairy at all, and that was when the Wildcats decided to crash the net.

One of their forwards was hammering at me as he stood in the blue paint. The puck appeared to have dribbled over the line right before I sat on it. The ref closest to me blew his whistle. The Wildcats had received a goaltender-interference penalty when everyone started shoving around in front of me. I'd simply skated away.

It was always what I did. I wasn't going to get into a fight with anyone. As Dave said, this is a mental game, and you have to make sure your head is in it all the time. You can't drift because of what the other team is trying to do to you, because what they're always *really* trying to do is throw you off your game.

Nothing else happened during that period. No goals, no close plays—just an endless back-and-forth. They threw everything they had at us in the third, but we knew how to sit on a one-nothing lead. We knew how to just keep it out of our end.

There wasn't another goal until the final minute. The Wildcats had pulled their goalie, and Jake spun and launched the puck high in the air toward the open net. The Wildcat defense chased the puck, but it was useless. The puck trickled in, and we had a two-nothing lead with only seconds left.

It felt good getting a shutout. But it felt even better that we had won the championship. We'd been the top team all year, so it wasn't a huge surprise. I felt for the other goalie though. In the end he had only let in one goal. But that's all it takes a lot of the time.

One goal.

I saw Principal Novak in the stands as we went to the handshake line. I hadn't noticed him during the game. But I never really look in the stands during a game. There was no nod of recognition. No thumbs-up for a good game. He shook a couple of people's hands, as though he had something to do with the win, and then pulled on his long black coat and left.

Chloe was there, sitting by herself. I noticed her watching me and raised my glove to her before the team tackled me.

Luke got MVP. It was well deserved. After a shutout you can always name the goalie player of the game, but if it hadn't been for the defense, I would have had to do a lot more work. And who knows, that one goal could have gone in on me.

That's the thing about being a goalie. You just can't make any mistakes.

"There it is, boys," Coach Ryan said. He clapped, and we all hooted and clapped along with him. The assistant coaches and other teachers who'd come into the locker room joined in. I could see Coach Ryan's eyes brimming. It was an emotional thing, winning a championship like this. All the hard work that went into it over the course of the term, all the early practices, the games, the dryland training. But we loved it. Every one of us.

We all loved winning. Who doesn't? We had pulled together and worked hard together for an entire season, and now here we were, the last ones standing.

Chloe was waiting for me in the lobby. You would think there'd be a lot of excitement in the lobby when we came out. But by the time we got out of the locker room, almost everyone had cleared out.

Chloe took my stick, and we walked through the doors and out into the freezing cold.

"Congratulations," she said.

"Thanks," I replied. I looked around. "You allowed to hang out with me?"

She didn't respond right away. "My parents are weird," she said.

"Even with all the evidence, even with Ella admitting what she did?"

"They still don't think I should have a steady boyfriend."

"What do you think?"

She grabbed my hand. "I think I can make these decisions myself."

Chapter Twenty

I always feel a little lost at the end of a season. It's been that way since I was in novice. But I move on to other things. I've never been huge on the whole "play hockey year round" idea. I play soccer and lacrosse. It feels good to get outside when the sun starts shining. But for those other months, the cold, dark ones, I wouldn't want to be anywhere else than on the ice.

The day after the finals, Chloe and I took Chubbs to the dog park near my house.

He loves to run around there with all the bigger dogs. Chloe and I sat on the bench and set him free. He came back right away three or four times before finally taking off to play.

"He's very needy," Chloe said. It was warm. We were still in our winter jackets, but we both had them unzipped. It wouldn't be long before the snow began to melt and the arenas closed down.

"He is," I said. "So where *do* your parents stand with everything now?"

"They have always had this strange belief that if someone gets busted for something, and they didn't do it, they *must* be guilty of something. They don't believe in coincidence."

"So you're still not telling them we're hanging out again?"

"I can do what I want. I'm sorry I ever listened to them."

Chubbs came over with a slobbery ball. He dropped it, and I kicked it away.

"I understand," I said. "Your parents don't make it easy."

"They sure don't." She held my hand then. We were both wearing mittens, but it didn't matter. "I'm really sorry all this happened to you."

"Me too."

"I can't excuse Ella. I can't even talk to her. We've been best friends since first grade and..."

"I know."

"It's just so bizarre." She sat there a long while not saying anything. "I see where it was coming from. But it was selfish."

"And weird."

"And hurtful."

"And really, really awful."

"I don't think I can forgive her," Chloe said. "I mean, maybe in time. But right now I can't see that time. She tried to ruin your reputation, she ruined my sets, and she destroyed our friendship. I don't think I can ever trust her again."

"I know I can't. But she's never really been a big fan of me." This was going to keep happening if Chloe and I continued to date. Not something as drastic as what had happened in the past few weeks. But her friends seemed unable to get past the stereotypes of jocks and artists and whatever other ones they'd created.

"You happy about the win?"

"Sure," I said. You'd think I'd sound more excited. But as I said, winning is expected, which is why losing is so hard.

"Champion!" Chloe said. "And now, on to the NHL so you can buy me that Porsche." She slid in close to me, and we watched Chubbs lose his mind barking at a husky that didn't seem to know he existed.

"Yeah, on to the NHL," I said. But I didn't really have that dream. When I was a kid it was there. I'd imagined myself playing for a Canadian team. Making a big save in game seven of the cup finals. But I realized somewhere along the line that making the NHL wasn't the point. Maybe it would happen—you never know. But I get the sense that skill isn't enough. You need luck too.

We stood and whistled for Chubbs. There was a light snow falling. It was little more than vapor in the air. Little crystals set off by the light of the sun.

Chubbs came to us covered in snow. I tried to brush him off, then gave up.

"What do you want to do this weekend?" Chloe asked. It was Monday. She was always planning ahead.

"Let's not go to a party," I said.

"Likely a good idea."

"Or a movie or a hockey game or a play."

"You're really cutting back on our options."

I didn't say anything else. I just wanted to be with her that weekend. Not doing anything. Not looking forward or back. Not talking about anything that had happened or making plans for the future. The past couple of weeks had been a roller coaster. My own private roller coaster. Or maybe more like a pinball machine when you suddenly have three balls going at once, everything coming at you, then drifting away.

I was never certain where, exactly, any of it was going to land.

Acknowledgments

Thanks to Tanya for yet another excellent edit. To all the staff at Orca Book Publishers for their hard work on every one of my novels. And to Dave Stathos, goalie coach extraordinaire, for inspiring young goaltenders and teaching how the mental game is just as important as the physical.

Jeff Ross is an award-winning author of several novels for young adults. He currently teaches scriptwriting and English at Algonquin College in Ottawa, Ontario, where he lives with his family. For more information, visit jeffrossbooks.com.

orca sports

For more information on all the books
in the Orca Sports series, please visit
orcabook.com.